MEDICINE
WALK

MEDICINE
WALK

by Ardath Mayhar

HOUGHTON MIFFLIN COMPANY BOSTON

Atlanta   Dallas   Geneva, Illinois   Palo Alto   Princeton   Toronto

Houghton Mifflin Edition, 1993

Printed in the U.S.A.

ISBN 0-395-61825-8

123456789-B-96 95 94 93 92

Contents

1 The Birthday Flight *3*

2 "First, You Think" *8*

3 The First Day *14*

4 Night by the Water *20*

5 The Second Day *28*

6 The Mile-Long Minute *36*

7 Toughing It *40*

8 Moon Visions *46*

9 "Keep Going, Burr!" *52*

10 Thinking It Out *57*

11 Feelings Don't Amount to Much *62*

12 The Trek of the Burr-Bot *68*

13 The Apache *72*

14 Grampa 77

Postscript *85*

MEDICINE
WALK

To Those Who Walk the Way

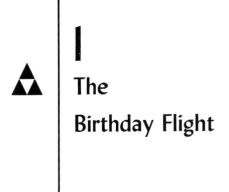

1
The
Birthday Flight

THE CESSNA'S TWIN ENGINES ROARED AS THE PLANE sped up the runway and banked into the sky. My heart was thumping in rhythm with them as we gained altitude. I almost felt as if I could soar out and fly beside the plane, to look down at our ranch, already shrinking to a tiny point below us.

I grinned at Dad. "This is going to be a great birthday!" I yelled above the noise of the engines. "Albuquerque! Grampa will have all the cousins there!" I thought with satisfaction that I would be the only one of the six who had reached the age of twelve. Dean wouldn't catch up until August. There would be all kinds of family fun and talking and games. Mom would have loved it . . . but I squashed that thought.

Dad's eyes crinkled at the corners, the way they do when he smiles, but his mouth was perfectly straight. "On a surprise visit? Aren't you being optimistic?" But he sounded so smug that I knew this visit wasn't going to be any total surprise.

I didn't answer. I turned to look over the wing, across the ridges of mountains. Before noon we'd be near the Mogollon Plateau. Maybe we'd even get a glimpse of Old Baldy later. I loved to fly, loved the feeling of freedom and speed it gave me. Dad didn't have that much time off from his medical practice, so we didn't get out together much. I intended to enjoy this trip to Albuquerque with every inch of me.

The morning droned away, and we stopped at noon to refuel. As usual, I made my pitch for angling off to the northeast to fly over the Petrified Forest. Usually we were on such a tight schedule that was out of the question. This time was different. Dad had a whole week off. He hadn't been feeling too well, and his partners had insisted on his taking a vacation. So this time he just might make my dream come true. Nachito, our foreman, ran our ranch anyway, so there was no reason why we two surviving Hendersons shouldn't take off into the blue, no strings attached. I gave a little bounce against the tension of my seat belt.

Dad grinned with his mouth this time. "Okay,

Burr. We'll be off our flight plan just a bit, but I guess it'll be all right. We'll go over the Apache Reservation. Interesting country. That's where Nachito was born and reared." He adjusted the compass heading, set the trim, and we headed out, farther north.

Though my gaze was fixed on the country below, I was thinking about Dad's words. Nachito was so old it was hard to believe he'd ever been a boy like Charlie, his grandson. That made me sort of understand some of the things Charlie was being trained to do. The old man must be trying to keep alive in his family some of the things he had learned from his tribe, growing up. That was why Charlie had to run five miles every morning before school.

It had seemed ridiculous to me, when Charlie told me about it. But there was something intriguing about it, too. I talked Charlie into letting me go with him one morning, and I was hooked. The air was cool and dusty. The land smelled alive and fresh. There was something about that run, besides being able (almost) to keep up with Charlie. I really saw and felt and smelled the land for the first time in my life. It had seemed as if a voice was talking to me, telling me secrets that I could nearly understand, secrets that only people who get out and set their feet on the earth, listen to the wind, taste the salt of their sweat ever get to know. I made a lot of runs after that.

My back cramped, and I sighed and shifted in my seat. It wouldn't be long now. The Cessna was purring, devouring the miles. We'd be over the forest, soon.

I heard something. Not loud enough to be heard over the engines, but pitched enough differently so it came through to me. I turned toward Dad in time to see him slump forward. His face was gray, his hands white-knuckled on the stick. Something in my chest gave a sick thump, and I went cold all over.

"Dad! What's wrong?" I leaned toward him and touched his shoulder. I could feel the tension in him.

He straightened a little. He was pale, with dark lines running from his nose to his mouth. He gripped the stick hard. "I'll . . . get us down," he grunted. "Be okay . . . when I get on . . . the ground." He was hurting. It showed in his face, sounded in his voice.

The nose dipped gently, and the Cessna went into a long glide. Below us were scrubby ridges full of irregular gullies. I knew I had to spot a smooth place to land, or we both were goners. But my hamburger from lunch kept trying to come up into my throat. I had to swallow it several times while I searched for some place to land.

"There!" I touched Dad's shoulder again and pointed off to our right. A long sandy space fanned out from the mouth of a dry wash.

He concentrated fiercely, banked the plane, lined up, lost altitude. We went in. Hard. The plane jounced and bumped. Things screeched and ground and flapped and rattled. Then we nosed over, as the wheels dug into the deep sand. Everything went terribly still.

I moved, felt along my bones. I was all right, I thought. "Any landing you can walk away from . . ." I began to say. Then I saw Dad's face.

He'd been flung forward, held by his belt. His head was turned sideways, toward me. His eyes were flat, all the sparkle gone from their gray depths. They were half open. His mouth was, too. He wasn't breathing. I wondered if he had been, that last desperate few hundred feet. But he'd brought me in alive.

I sat still, feeling stunned. Something cold and sick curled up inside me.

"Dad! Dad!" But I knew he wouldn't answer. Couldn't answer.

I took his wrist between my thumb and finger and felt for a pulse, the way he'd taught me. There wasn't even a flutter.

Dad was dead.

2

"First,
You Think"

THAT GREASY, COLD THING COILED AND SHIFTED IN MY
gut. Suddenly I was terribly, horribly sick. I bent
forward, the belt cutting into my middle, and threw
up all over the rudder pedals at my feet. Something
trickled down my forehead, then, and I knew I'd hit
something as we went in. I took the towel Dad kept
in the cockpit and wiped first my forehead, then my
mouth. I almost used some of the metal two-quart
bottle of water to rinse out with, then I thought. I
might just need water worse later than I did now.

Sand was piled up in front of the windscreen, so
I couldn't see ahead at all. I took the mike of the radio
down and thumbed the button. "Mayday, Mayday.
This is silver Cessna Number NA 20364, down northeast of the Mogollons." There wasn't a sound. Not

a crackle of static, no hum. The radio was as dead as
. . . Dad. I jerked myself up short. This was no time
for going all mushy. Dad would be the first to say it,
too. He and Nachito had always seen eye to eye on
the subject of self-control.

I unsnapped my seat belt and turned to the
door. The sun, through its window, was high, blazing
against the sand just behind us. We were in shadow,
for the plane had plowed forward between the gully's
banks. Bushes and trees hung over, making dense
shade where I sat. All my careful instructions were
useless. Staying with the plane wouldn't gain me
anything, for we not only were hidden from the air,
but also off our flight plan.

I'd have to walk out. I'd need a hat. The only
one in the plane was Dad's. I leaned over and touched
his face. It was warm, but not with a tingle that had
life to it. Simply, that wasn't Dad anymore. The
thing that had made him himself was gone. I swallowed hard, tasting vomit, and moved his head forward as gently as I could. I pulled at his khaki hat,
which was caught between his head and the far side
of the cockpit. When I had it loose, I held his head
for a moment. The tears almost got away from me
that time, and I laid the brown curls back against the
wall.

I knew I ought to bury him. That was what you

did with dead people, as I knew all too well. But Dad had been a big man, heavy boned. And for all my strength, I was only twelve, half his size or less. I'd never be able to move him out of the plane. And if I did, what was the use of burying him in sand, where he'd be washed away in the spring runoff?

Dad had loved the 310. It was his pride and joy. It would make a good coffin for him, I thought. And once I had wedged the doors shut, wild animals couldn't get to him, either.

I unlatched the door beside me and pushed hard. It was partly sprung, and I had a hard job of it for a minute. But once I had my feet on the ground, I kept standing there staring up at Dad, feeling lower than I've ever felt in my life. I knew I had to go, but I also knew that once I left the plane, everything would change forever. While I stood here, even with Dad slumped as he was, things seemed kind of normal. I pushed myself away with both hands. He had put his last strength into saving me, and I had to make good on that.

"I've got to go, Dad. But I remember everything you taught me. First you think: That's what you dinged into me all my life. And I will. I'm going to make it out of here. For you. For Mom." I choked for a moment. "Say hello to Mom for me, will you? Give her my l—" But then I couldn't go on.

Fighting tears, I reached behind the seats and

pulled out the emergency gear, and then I latched the door and wedged it with sticks, which I set into a pile of stones.

When that was done, I sat in the shade and looked at what I had to survive with. A bottle of water, maybe two quarts. Some dried fruits. A flashlight. First-aid materials. Rope. Too much to carry, with the kind of country I had to cross.

I emptied out the supply bag and started over again. The bottle of water went in. The raisins and apricots. The flashlight, whose batteries seemed terribly weak. Iodine, sterile bandages, the snakebite kit, the scissors. The rest, with the rope, had to stay. Carrying too much would just wear me out.

Then I rested a little while, hating to leave the relatively cool shade for the sun-baked ridges. I set my chin in my hands and for some reason Nachito's face swam into my thoughts.

"In the old days there was nothing for the Apache except for the things the land provided," his reedy old voice was saying. "Even those were not given freely, without effort. But the People were strong and determined, and they lived. I am teaching Charlie to live, too, for the White Man's world will not always be here. The land and the People will. If you listen to the land, respect her and her gifts, you will be able to overcome anything."

I shook myself and sat straight. It made a lot of

sense, hallucination or not. A pound of raisins and twelve ounces of apricot halves were not going to take me far, and I was at least forty miles from any-where, though I hadn't a clue as to where I might be. I had to go up and down the ranges of mountains until I came to something. It was a good thing I had run with Charlie; I was tough as whipcord, for what that was worth. If I made it out, it would be because of the training I had shared, a bit, with Charlie.

Nachito's face came into my mind again. "Noth-ing comes easy in this country. Everything costs dearly, though not in money. But you can do any-thing, if you try hard enough. In the old days, a warrior could run a hundred miles in a day. He would begin with a mouthful of water. After he had run for twenty miles or so, he would swallow it and keep running. He expected nothing, and so he was not disappointed when nothing was given him."

Water. That was going to be a problem. Even if I found streams, they'd probably be dried up. Food wasn't too big a worry. I wasn't fat, but I had eaten well all my life. It takes a long time to starve. I'd been shown some edible grubs and plants, too, if I got desperate. Water would be the main thing. And sit-ting there in the shade wasn't using what I had to advantage. Nachito would have been two miles on his way, by now.

I looked toward the plane. Light reflected from the windows so I couldn't see Dad's shape inside. I pulled myself to my feet and tightened the cord on the khaki hat so it wouldn't fall down around my ears. Then I settled it on my head and looked up at the sun.

If I remembered the big map at the last airport, the nearest town would be Holcomb, somewhere off to the east. If I headed east, I'd have to run into roads eventually, at the very least. Flying, it wouldn't be more than fifty miles or so. Clambering around in the gullies and over the ridges, I'd probably have to cover a hundred to make it out. A long way.

I trudged through the sand, onto the rocky slope, and looked back at the plane for one last time. The shadows dappled it, camouflaging it.

Deep in my gut there was a lost space. An emptiness.

"Bye, Dad," I whispered, ashamed of the sentimentality of it.

Then I put my back to the sun and began to walk.

3
The
First Day

THE MORNING WAS HOT. THE AIR WAS THIN AND DRY, and the sky was a faded blue that promised no relief. I had spent my first night huddled into a cranny in another of the dry washes that seemed to runnel the whole area. I'd been as cold then as I was hot now. There was a hogback ridge ahead. Again. I seemed to do nothing but climb up or climb down. I was one huge ache. A dry ache.

I was thirsty . . . more than thirsty, but I didn't touch the bottle. I wasn't doing so well as those old Apache, not by a long shot. I had taken a mouthful early and maybe traveled a mile before I swallowed it. I hoped to do a lot better next time. Just having water in my mouth helped a lot. It held off the raspy-throated feeling; my tongue didn't behave like used sandpaper. At noon I'd take another mouthful and try to hold it half the afternoon. If I could.

I was moving carefully, checking for loose rock and unexpected holes. A broken leg would mean the end, out here. Still, even that was getting to be automatic, and my mind kept wandering off, spinning strange notions.

Mom drifted out of a clump of rock up ahead. She was wearing the blue jumpsuit she liked best. In her hands was a glass of lemonade. "Hurry, Burr! It'll get warm before you drink it!" she was urging me. I could see her bronze hair moving in the breeze. Her bandana, stuck in her hip pocket, was fluttering, too.

I almost let go and ran to her, but I caught myself. That wasn't here and now. That was the morning of the awful day. I had run, then, grabbed the glass and gulped down the liquid. She'd tousled my hair with her strong fingers and said, "Want to go with me, old chum? It's going to be an exciting show, and your Aunt Martha would love for you to be there."

I had grinned at her over the rim of the glass. "Yeah. I know how much she likes my comments on her paintings. Thanks, Mom, but no thanks. I like pictures, but I hate fine art. Or maybe I just don't like the kind of people who go to things like that. I'd rather stay here and go scavenging with Charlie."

She had laughed, that deep chuckle that always made me feel good inside. "I don't really blame you. The arty ones turn me off, too. But Martha would be hurt if I didn't show up. Have fun, and don't get snakebit!"

I hadn't even kissed her goodbye. That still rankled, deep down inside where nobody knew it but me. And before she got to town a truck creamed her little sports car.

I shook my head, hard and came to, standing on the rocky slope. I didn't need that kind of thing. I had to keep my mind on what I was doing, not go wandering around in a daze, daydreaming. That was a good way to get killed, and I knew it all too well.

At noon I paused on top of a ridge. There was a stunted piñon growing there, and I thought of something Nachito had told me. I pulled a handful of the fragrant needles and tucked them into my pocket. One I put into my mouth and chewed. The acid taste made my mouth water, which was all to the good. A cheap drink, though not very satisfying. Still, it was enough to let me swallow a small pinch of raisins and half an apricot. I left the bottle untouched. It was a matter of pride, now.

I angled down the other side of the ridge. Its twin loomed ahead, and I groaned. All the relatives who had visited us had raved over the mountains in Arizona. It was sure and certain that they hadn't had to walk over them. Not only was it exhausting, but I was having trouble keeping directions straight in my head, what with all the going up and down and back and forth, finding passable places. I must have traveled twelve or fifteen miles since I set out, but I probably hadn't gone more than five miles east. If that.

I lucked into a game trail about halfway down the ridge. It meandered among the rocky ledges, but it was better than trying to find a way down the steep slope with no guide at all. I was stepping along, half in a dream again and fussing at myself about it, when I heard a buzzing rattle.

I froze. Where was it? I turned my eyeballs in their sockets, not moving anything else. Right to left. Back again. There! Up ahead, its dusty colors hiding it against the baked rock and dust of the trail, was a diamond-back. Its head was forward, forked tongue testing the air. Its tail was quivering furiously.

I hate snakes. I'm not exactly afraid of them; something in my inside just squirms when I see the way they move. But I was afraid of this one. To be bitten, out here alone, would be bad. Fatally bad.

Something popped into my mind. Charlie handled snakes. Live ones, rattlers and all. He had never been bitten. What was it Nachito had told him? I could see the seamed, saddle-colored face, the narrow squinted eyes, as the old man oiled harness leather and talked, while we polished bits and stirrups.

"The snake, he is a part of the land. He is wise, in his own way, and he is dangerous, for he knows only his own way. A man knows more than a snake. He can cow a snake, if he doesn't smell of fear. A serpent knows one thing: a fearful man is dangerous to him. He will strike if he smells fear on you. But if you are not afraid . . . not a little bit . . . you can calm him. You can make him wonder, deep in that small, strange brain, what it is that you are and can do. And then you are the winner."

That had been something Nachito had worked out for himself, I thought, for none of the Apache hands seemed to know about it. But it sounded as if it might be true. Nachito usually knew what he was talking about.

I stared at the long, coiled shape. I made myself relax, muscle by muscle, without moving a peg. My nerves quit jumping and lay quiet. My breathing eased. My hands unclenched. The snake's head lowered to a point just above the first coil. The buzz changed its pitch.

The diamond-back wasn't a horrible-looking creature, once you thought about it. It was beautiful, in its own way. Strong and sleek, patterned in subdued colors just right for its world. And the poison; it was no worse than my own ability to pick up a stick and smash the creature flat.

I looked into the serpent's eyes. It lowered its head even more. I didn't blink, but set my will against that of the snake. I urged it with all my might to go on about its business among the rocks. The rattle rasped irritably.

Time crawled past. The sun moved slowly down toward the top of the ridge high above, though I didn't spare much thought for it. And at last the snake began uncoiling. It curled its head about as if looking for a direction. I willed harder than ever, sweat pouring off me—from the sun, now, not from fear. And the rattler slid away among the rocks.

My knees felt weak. My heart was pounding, but not with fear. I'd been working harder, those past minutes, than ever before in my life. And I'd won! A feeling of triumph swept over me. Nachito had been right! And I'd been able to use his words to make myself unafraid. If I could do this much, maybe I just might make it!

My head was light with relief when I went on. The trail eased down, into the cooler bowl of shadow that was the eastern slope of the ridge, safe now from the sun. I picked up my pace as the going grew easier.

I smelled water!

4

Night
by the Water

BETWEEN THE RIDGE I'D JUST COME DOWN AND THE
toes of the neighboring mesa ran a narrow valley. At
its bottom there was a wide streambed with a trickle
of water snaking down its middle. Cottonwoods were
growing along the banks, and scrub and few piñons
lined its course.

I badly wanted to run the rest of the way. But
I'd been walking over this kind of terrain for a while
now. I knew the sort of trap it could set for a foot
that wasn't very careful. I held myself back by main
force, but I did fumble for the water bottle and drain
it into my mouth.

Something inside me perked up to attention.
"That was a foolish thing," it said to me, almost
in a real voice. "What if the water down there is

alky-water? What if it's polluted so you can't drink it? What'll you do then? And now you've spoiled your control. You'll have to start all over again."

It wasn't exactly me talking, way down there inside myself. It was partly Nachito's teachings, partly my listening to the tales the Apache hands told and to Charlie's family stories. This wasn't my own country. My kind had never had to face it, raw, the way the Apache had. But the Apache were human beings, no more, no less. What they could learn to do, surely I could—if I had the time left before a rattler or the sun or thirst got me. But I knew how lucky I was to have shared even a little of Charlie's training. It gave me a handle on things that I'd never have been able to work out for myself.

Now I was almost on a level with the cotton-woods. A track led across the streambed to the water. I chanced running until I was on that path, and then I looked down. Prints, not of cattle. Dainty. Mule deer, I thought. Even with the shadows of late evening blurring them, I could trace the narrow outlines; but there was another, too. I stared down with my spine curling back on itself. A cat track, bigger than my spread hand, fingers and all. A shiver went up me and then back down.

I paused right there, thinking hard. It seemed there was plenty of game. That fellow shouldn't be hungry. I had no reason to think it might develop a taste for me. But I was alone, and I was relatively small. Maybe just about the right size for a midnight snack! Who knew what any wild animal might be thinking? Nachito had taught me caution, along with so much else.

I went down to the water a lot more carefully than I might have. At the brushy border of the vegetation, I stopped dead still and looked hard up and down the stream. There were a lot of tracks out on the flat, outlined in shadow on the dun-colored sand and pebbles. I listened, then. Something went crashing through the brush across and upstream from me, but I didn't see anything. There came a splash from upstream, where a bend in the watercourse had formed an eddy. I could see a large hole of water. It looked pretty deep.

Maybe a fish? That would come in handy in the morning, if I could get him out. I looked about one more time and stepped into the open, then moved up along the shallow stream toward that deep place.

A bird called shrilly, somewhere out of sight. A sad, keening cry echoed down the valley. A shiver went back over the course, leaving goosepimples in its wake. I thought of that cat track.

Something rustled in one of the cottonwoods, making a *wheerp?* sound. Eerie. This was different

country from my own, down in the southwest corner
of the state. I didn't know what kinds of creatures I
might find here.

I was almost to the pool. Just as the light died
away I got there. The water shone silvery under the
starlight. I ached to feel it lapping against my skin,
and I sat on a rock and pulled off my sneakers, if you
could call them that any more. Tatters would probably be a better word for them. But I wanted to soak
my bruised, cut, scraped, sore feet. Not to mention
the rest of me, which felt as if I'd been living on a
griddle.

Still, I had to drink and fill my bottle before I
fouled the water. I made it take a while . . . didn't
want to lose control again. My mouth was aching for
a scoop of that chilly water, but I made it wait while
I filled the bottle and capped it, bent again, very
slowly, and made a cup of my hands. Then I drank.
There's nothing, just absolutely nothing, as good as
plain cold water. If you don't believe me, just try
staggering up and down mountains for a while without enough of it.

When I was through, I skinned out of my T-shirt
and jeans and underwear and slid into the pool. The
air was getting chilly now, but my sunburn didn't
really know that. I sat on the bottom of the pool with
my head sticking out. It eased the burn a lot, and I

sat there long after I was cold. Something about the water made me feel better, inside as well as outside.

But when I closed my eyes, all I could see was Dad's face as it had been when I saw it last. It seemed to be engraved on the insides of my eyelids. I opened my eyes again quickly. Something inside me was holding away the fact that Dad was dead. I couldn't afford that kind of grief, the full realization of what I'd lost. Not now. I didn't have the strength and energy to spare. I had to turn my feelings all the way off, the way the Apache had done. Cold and tough and unfeeling, that was the only way I could come out of this alive.

I shook myself, standing in the water, then waded ashore. It was cold now, and my teeth chattered as I stripped the water off my skin with my hands. I pulled on my gritty clothes with shaking hands, welcoming the faint warmth of the sand around my feet. The rocks were even warmer, and the big boulder on which I'd sat glowed with heat. I thought for a minute of digging myself into the sand around the base of that rock. Then I remembered the cat track.

The moon wasn't up yet, but it wasn't too dark. The sky was full of stars, the Milky Way a shining bar. My eyes had adjusted as the light left, so I could see fairly well. I could find someplace safer to sleep,

I thought. A gruff cough from upstream made me hurry into the line of cottonwoods.

Looking up, I could see them outlined against the sky. I needed one with branches big enough for me to feel secure. I had to sleep if I was to cover any distance tomorrow. Sleeping in a tree was never one of my ambitions, but it was a darn sight better than waking up in the jaws of a cougar. Long ago Dad and I had made a trip into the Rockies. Our guide had told us hair-curlers about campers being torn out of their sleeping bags by bears. I felt sure that what a bear could do, a cougar could do . . . and better.

A tree up ahead leaned against the one next to it, making a kind of stair. I moved to it, felt it. The roots were out of the ground, but the wood was alive, and the tree it leaned against had good-sized branches. I went up like a monkey and pulled myself onto a solid limb.

I wouldn't call it a comfortable place to sleep. Still, there was one limb that I could wrap my arms around and lean my head on while I sat on the one below. I wouldn't fall out. It would do.

As I settled onto my perch, something moved on the path below. Quiet sounds, moving toward the water. Deer, maybe, or elk, going to drink. Something squalled in the distance, and the hooves stilled. Echoes bounced crazily around the canyon. When

they died, the steps below went on; and I settled my
head onto my arm and tried my best to relax.

My stomach growled painfully, and I sat up,
surprised at myself. I'd forgotten about eating. I must
be getting used to being hungry, or else I was so
worried about that cougar off in the brush that I
didn't think. I maneuvered my pack around in front
of me and dug out a handful of raisins. When they
were gone, I got out half an apricot and ate that, too.
They went down into a huge pit of emptiness and
got lost there.

When my "meal" was over, I got into position
again, but sleep wouldn't come. I was thinking, for
the first time, about how different I was from the
person I'd been a day and a half ago. Last night I'd
been too bone tired, too shocked and exhausted, to
do anything but curl up in a rock cranny and sleep.
Now I felt odd—lightheaded, almost above myself,
looking down with surprise at the Burr Henderson
in the cottonwood.

I'd never in my life gone without eating all I
wanted, drinking all I needed, sleeping in a comfortable bed after a refreshing shower. I'd never really
believed that you could do without such things.
Books told about people who didn't have what I had,
but books were removed from the person I really
was. Now I knew they were true. I knew that you

could live with practically nothing and keep going.

I'd found a space inside myself that I'd never suspected was there. I was finding that I knew things I hadn't realized I knew. Part of it came from Nachito and the Apache hands. Part came from watching Dad on camping and hunting and canoeing trips, before he got so busy, and listening to his tales and explanations. But a big lot of it was just there: things I never remember knowing or being told.

I stared into the night. "Maybe inside every one of us is a Stone Age man, just waiting to be needed," I said aloud. Then I grinned. Who'd believe I was sitting in a tree talking to myself, out in the middle of nowhere?

I was only half asleep when the cougar padded to the foot of my tree, sniffed around for a terribly long time, then finally turned away and left. Only then did I relax totally and drop into a sleep so deep that the tree might have been my bed at home.

5

The
Second Day

I WOKE SUDDENLY, BEWILDERED, FEELING THE PAIN-
ful crease across my butt where the limb had pressed
into me all night. I lifted my head and found that my
arms had gone numb; my hands felt like lumps of
mud. As I worked to get my fingers moving again,
I listened. Something had awakened me.

Light was just showing in the sky behind the
mesa to the east. A bird, calling downstream, was
answered by another in a nearby cottonwood. Then
there came again the sound that had awakened me. A
snarling scream rang between the heights on either
hand, echoing back and forth, filling the dawn with
fear. The cougar.

I squirmed around to put the branch beneath a
different part of my anatomy. My hands were work-

ing well enough now to dig out a few more raisins, which I tried to chew and couldn't. A tiny sip of water eased things a bit, and I managed to get them down, along with another piece of apricot. When I was done, my teeth felt as if they had fur overcoats. I broke off a twig and chewed it the way Nachito had showed me, making it into a brush of scrubby wood fibers. With this I polished my teeth. It tasted terrible, but I felt a lot better.

By then it was light. The stream looked flat and pewter-colored, and the trees and rocks were dark cutouts against it, but day was definitely at hand. I climbed down without bothering with the slanted trunk, dropping the last seven feet or so. On the ground I shifted my pack once more and eased off toward the water. If that had been a fish jumping the night before, I just might be able to catch it. Dad had taught me some pretty useful skills on our jaunts together.

I crept forward, moving as quietly as Nachito had tried to teach me to do. The eddy swirled slowly, catching the growing light in round ripples. I lay on my stomach and wormed forward until my face was just edged over the flat rock at the water's edge, then squinted down through the silvery ripples. There were rounded pebbles on the bottom, shadows among shadows. But one was darker . . . shaped like a fish.

It was lying along the bottom, motionless. Asleep? I hoped so.

I slipped my hands into the water, feeling the icy ripples begin to numb them. One hand on either side, deep enough but not too deep . . . then bring them together slowly, gently, as if they were bits of weed drifting in the current. That was the way. I grabbed, and the fish convulsed; but it was too late. I had him.

It was shaped like a trout, but there were differences I didn't recognize. I didn't care. It was food. Before it had stopped its reflexive flopping, I had it gutted and scaled with the pocket knife that had been one of Dad's birthday presents to me.

I had no matches, and I wasn't about to try making fire with a fire stick. I ate it raw. It tasted wonderful. Not delicious, you understand. Just plain wonderful. I could feel my body soaking up the raw flesh like a sponge.

I didn't waste any time after that. Before the sun was above the mountaintops, I was off again, while it was cool and I still had energy. The stream angled off southeastward, following the prevailing slant of all the mountain ranges in this part of the country. Near enough to my direction, I thought. For me a straight line was definitely not the shortest distance, not with climbing up and down and getting into bottlenecks and having to backtrack. By following the water I could cover more ground faster, as well as have a supply of drinking water right at hand. There would also be shade, if I needed it.

I still think it was a good idea and would have worked, if things had gone a bit differently. But a couple of miles down the canyon a wall of rubble choked off the way. Though the water seemed to be finding a course through the mess, it was too loose and shifty for me to dare try it. And it plugged the passage between two overhanging cliffs. There was no going around, either. Those cliffs were not only sheer, they were undercut in places. No way to climb them that I could see.

I had to go back a half mile or more before I found a possible way up. A chimney had been carved down through the rock by some fault, or maybe a stream of runoff water. It looked narrow enough to go up, if I could remember the methods Dad had told about using in his climbing days.

I took a drink of water and refilled my bottle as full as it would go. Then I tackled the cranny. It was already hot, though the sun was only now lighting the far wall of the canyon. Inside the cranny it was *really* hot.

By now my tennies were hardly more than scraps of fabric tied around my ankles. My feet were unmentionable. I left the bits of tops on just to keep from blistering any more than necessary. Working my way up that narrow cut, feet on one side, back against the other, was torture for everything I owned. I even discovered parts I hadn't known I had, and they hurt, too. But I had lucked out in one way—the crack was not too wide for the length of my legs. It was possible. Not easy, but possible.

If you wonder why I didn't just go back to the place where I spent the night and go up the easier slope there, you just don't understand the state of my feet. To force them back up that pebbly stream-bed, covering ground already spotted with more than a few drops of my own blood, was a thing I couldn't do. So I set my back and my feet and hunched upward.

From time to time I looked up. The cranny was irregular, leaning this way and that, but I could see a wink of blue at its top. It came out above.

By the time I'd gone up fifteen or twenty feet, I thought the skin was probably entirely off my back. I tried to forget about my feet. And there wasn't any relief in sight. I had to go up, or go back. I kept plugging, through a sort of frozen time when my body kept moving according to instructions, and my mind free-wheeled.

What had hit me, all of a sudden, was the kind of a fix I was in. I had never dreamed of ever being entirely alone, without a human being to call on for help. Dad had always been at the end of a phone call.

Nachito had been at hand. Charlie had been with me, most of the time except for nights. Now there was nobody. Nobody at all even knew where I was or that I was still alive. It was the scariest thought I had ever had in all my twelve years and two days.

I turned off my mind and didn't think about anything but the creased stone across from my eyes, the feel of the rock against my back and elbows and hands. The pack was a pain too, though I had shifted it around to ride on my belly.

About fifty feet up, I came to a place where there was enough purchase to let me look down. That was a mistake. I started shivering. That morning's raw fish tried to come up into my throat. I jerked my gaze back to the rockwall and *moved*. The remnants of my sneakers looked positively beautiful.

After a long time I came to a bit of outcrop. It was a pain to work my way around it, and once that was done I decided to set my shoulders on it and rest a little. I needed to eat a few raisins, anyway. My energy was going fast. And I had to get out into open country with enough zip left in me to signal to any plane that might be searching for our downed aircraft.

As if the mere thought had called it up, there came a distant drone. A plane, no doubt of that. And there was no way on earth he could see me, down in this crack. I strained upward, trying to see up the chimney, but it was no use. I felt sicker than before.

Tears rose into my eyes and a couple escaped before I could pull them back. I shook myself and got ready to start again. It seemed that this was going to be up to me, all the way.

I stepped up with feet, scootched up with my back, stepped up again, over and over. My mind kept wandering around and having to be pulled up short before it reached dangerous territory. I tried to keep it steered away from Dad, from Mom and Grampa and Dean and the rest of the cousins. Thinking about them would make me feel soft and squishy, and that wasn't anything I could afford, right now.

I thought of Nachito and Charlie. That was better . . . nothing squishy about either of them. Charlie had told me all about the medicine journey he was due to take when he got to be twelve. I'd felt envious of him, having a ritual so old and tough and unusual ahead of him. In six months he'd be off on that walk. He had to go out into the wilderness, all alone, without food or water, and find the guiding spirit for his life. His symbol. His totem.

I paused for a moment, my feet braced. I was twelve. Was this my own medicine journey? It had all the earmarks, that was sure. I had been twelve the very day it started. I had next to no food, and very little water. I had already done things I'd never dreamed myself capable of doing.

"I might just die," I said aloud, and the words echoed eerily up the chimney. I hadn't let myself think about that much. But now it wasn't too scary. I'd been doing my very best, step by step. Maybe everything hadn't been *right*, but it had been the best I knew how to do at the time. Was this the way a medicine walk was supposed to go?

I didn't know. I wasn't Apache, or even Indian. Things probably wouldn't go for me the way they would for Charlie.

I looked up, gauging the distance, and began moving again. I was almost halfway up, the best I could judge, but it still looked like a terribly long way to the top. I was tired. I couldn't recall ever having been so tired. My knees were beginning to tremble, along with my arms. I was panting, though I tried to control that. My T-shirt was not only ragged but absolutely filthy with sweat and grit.

I maneuvered around another knob of rock at my back. It was about time! I needed another resting perch. I settled back against it to get my breath.

Without any warning, the rock shifted and fell away with a grinding clatter. Suddenly my shoulders were lower than my feet, and my heavier upper half wanted to follow the rock down the chimney.

My heart gave a tremendous thump.

This is it, I thought. Now is when I die.

6

The

Mile-Long Minute

THE WORLD FROZE. TIME SEEMED TO STOP. THE COLD calm that I'd been able to hold since Dad died deserted me entirely, and I screamed. The long wail echoed back at me for seconds after I'd stopped. Fresh sweat streamed down me, and this was not from heat. It was from sheer terror. I could feel those rocks down there, chewing me to hamburger when I hit.

From somewhere the calm slipped into me again. I saw Nachito's face. He didn't say anything, just looked at me with that measuring expression he used so often on Charlie and me.

My feet were firm on the far wall. I felt with my hands for some fingerhold to reinforce the friction of my shoulders against the rock. There was nothing. Even the socket the rock had slipped from slanted the wrong way, downward, useless. Sweat from my hair was dripping down the shaft as I paused and breathed very slowly. It was time to think.

Now I heard a voice. Not Nachito's. Not mine. And not with my ears: They heard only the rasp of a breeze against the rocks. The voice said, "A man does not wait to die." It had a growly tone, inhuman. "One who finds himself in a terrible place finds his way out again. He uses his mind and his spirit. He listens to the wind and the stones and the water. If he thinks like the land, the plants, the trees . . . but you are not of the People. Perhaps you cannot."

I found that I'd closed my eyes. Now I opened them. How did you think like a plant or listen to a rock? And who did that . . . whoever . . . think he was, telling me that I wasn't a person?

I felt the stone opposite with my toe. I'd put that foot up there. I had to get it down again.

I slid my foot downward and set it firmly. The other one now . . . right there. Now I was almost level, knees bent, shoulders more secure against the rock. I tried moving my shoulders up, but the angle was still wrong. I stopped and reset my feet still lower. Then I rested. That had been the longest minute of my entire life.

Once I had the feet below the shoulders, I was in a position from which I could move upward again.

I didn't rest on any more rocks, no matter how tired I got or how convenient they seemed. I hunched and pushed and scrabbled my way up the chimney. A time came when I could have reached the rim, just above my head, but I didn't try. I went caterpillaring upward until my head came out the hole. Only then did I grab the stony outcrop of the edge and heave myself out of the crack.

Far away, down in the canyon, I heard the gravelly "yeoooorwch!" of a cougar. Shivering, I crawled to the rim to look down. There was a tawny flicker of motion as something flashed across the threadlike stream and into the cottonwoods.

"What is he doing hunting by day?" I asked a chipmunk that had been watching me with cautious alertness since I'd emerged from the very earth at its feet.

I didn't pretend to be an expert on big cats. Maybe some kinds hunted by day.

The sun was at an angle that said it was just past noon. Considering everything, I hadn't made bad time. Now I had to get into the shade. Dad's khaki hat was at the bottom of the shaft, and I wasn't about to go back after it.

Something occurred to me, and I laughed, though it came out pretty cracked. In a thousand years, maybe, an archeologist might dig up that hat and wonder how and why it was where it was. That was the kind of joke Dad would appreciate.

Then I thought of Grampa's handkerchief trick. He was bald in the middle of his head, and his scalp blistered easily. Whenever he was unexpectedly caught out in the sun, he would take his handkerchief and tie knots in all four corners, making a sort of cap for himself.

I dug into my hip pocket and brought out my own handkerchief. I hadn't ever been known for clean handkerchiefs, and this one had seen its best days a good long while before. It was so dirty it was hard to tell it had ever been a handkerchief, but I knotted the corners and put the oddball creation on my head. It dulled the worst of the heat.

Then I rose and went to the edge of the small space near the rim. A gnarled piñon stood there. I thought wistfully of piñon nuts, but it was the wrong time of the year for them. Although my stomach had stopped growling long, long before, my bones felt light and hollow, and I knew it was from lack of food.

I went into the shade of the piñon and leaned against its rough bark. Though I was still shaking a bit from my near-disaster in the shaft, it didn't matter. As soon as I'd rested a little, I knew that I was going on.

7

Toughing It

IT WAS AFTER NOON . . . AROUND TWO, I THOUGHT from examining the angle of the sun. My watch hadn't survived the scraping it got in the shaft, so I couldn't be certain. I missed knowing what time it was, not that it would have done me any good. I remembered Nachito's scorn for white men's fixation on watches and clocks.

"Do you make a day a minute longer by knowing the time? What is it, this time that you know? It is not the rock's time or the sun's time or the chipmunk's time. It is a thing the white has made up. He uses it to control his fellows. It is no good to anyone who lives by the world as it is."

As I rose and moved along the top of the cliff, I thought about that. It's true, you know. Here I had

no school to go to, no doctor or dentist who had to
have me in his office at the precise time he'd scheduled
for me. Here time might not exist at all, just day and
night, cold and hot, wet and dry. Mostly dry.

As I struggled among the rocks and ridges, I felt
that I had lived for years and years since the minute
when I knew that Dad was sick. I was so much older
now than I had been then that my twelfth birthday
might have been years instead of days behind me.

There was a path leading back into skimpy trees.
I followed it, watching where I put my feet. The sun
was hot, and the snakes would be moving—rattlers. If
they were like the first, they'd be big ones.

This mesa was almost bald on top, like Grampa.
The upper part had looked smooth as a table from
the top of the opposite ridge, but it was uneven, gul-
lied and stony. The sun was terrible, and the effort
of walking made me even hotter.

I wished that I had waited among the piñons at
the canyon's edge until the sun went lower. It would
have been cooler, and I'd have made better time without taking the risk of giving myself a heatstroke.

I stopped beside an upthrust of rock and took
out the water bottle. Not to drink—I had pretty good
control of that, now. Instead, I put a tiny bit of water
on my handkerchief-hat and squeezed it together,
dampening the whole thing somewhat. When I re-

placed it, the breeze made by my motion evaporated the water, and my head was cooler. It was a relief, while it lasted, and I trudged onward. But I knew I was overheating; a reddish mist was rising behind my eyes.

A couple of days before I'd have dropped down to the gritty mesa-top and said, "I can't go another step!" I'd have meant it; and it would have been true. Now I was someone else, someone who didn't think of stopping. There was nothing to stop for. I could die here and now, or I could keep going and die trying.

That reminded me of Dad. I could hear his voice: "I'll do that, or I'll die trying!" Now I knew what Dad had meant. He was that kind of man. He *had* died trying. I thought maybe that original moment in the plane would have killed an ordinary man, one who didn't have the will to save his only son.

That was what a man did . . . or a woman. Mom hadn't been a bit different. That was what real *people* did, kept on and on, no matter what. Now I might be able to prove to Nachito that I was as strong and determined as his People were. Not that the old man would ever know . . . or would he?

I thought about that as I put one foot ahead of the other. Maybe he would. He had his ways, Nachito.

Even the other Apache looked at him with awe when one of his predictions turned out to be right on the button.

"I listen to the rock. I listen to the wind. I listen to the plants. They tell me things nobody else can hear, for no one else listens," he used to say. Maybe these rocks and the few bushes and the wind might carry word to him about how Burr Henderson died.

I shook myself, and the red haze lessened a little. I'd been walking along in a daze or a dream. I'd been hallucinating, I thought. Heat and exhaustion could cause that. I wasn't a doctor's son for nothing. I'd forgotten to eat again, too.

I stopped in the middle of a stride and looked up at the sun. A crazy impulse made me shout at the burning shield in the sky, "What should I do? Just tell me, and I'll do it!"

Okay. Tell me I'm crazy. Tell me I was hallucinating. The breeze whispered right into my ears, "Resssst . . ." In twenty more steps I found myself staring down into a deep gully. The sun was down far enough so that one side of it was in shadow. It looked as deep and dark as a Black Hole.

I looked up toward the sun, then down into that refuge. "Thanks," I croaked.

I scrambled down the cleft and leaned against the rock. It was cooler than the air. Just to be out of the sun was wonderful, too. I sipped one swallow of water, chewed on a few raisins. They were hard to swallow, for my throat wasn't wet enough, but I managed without taking any more water. Then I sat and leaned, closing my eyes and letting my mind relax.

I could feel my backbone grating against the stone. I'd lost a lot of weight; all that climbing and walking would have done that, even with enough to eat and drink. I dug into the bag, eyes still closed, and pulled out half an apricot. Not many left. Few raisins were left, either. When those were gone, then what?

I chewed the bits of apricot and the raisins slowly, savoring every scrap. Twenty times I chewed each bite, playing the game Mom had taught me when I was little. But everything was gone too soon, and I put the bag into a cranny in the rock. I intended to sleep, even if it meant that I'd never wake up again. With some sleep, I might be able to walk a good long way in the night hours. Snakes or no snakes, the sun was more dangerous.

I didn't know I'd been asleep until I woke again.

The cougar roused me as its growly screech echoed among the cliffs on either side. It brought me to my feet before I was more than half awake.

It was dark, fully dark. After midnight. The

waning moon was halfway up the east . . . not a lot of light, but enough to help. Maybe I could manage to keep my sense of direction, with the moon in the east. I couldn't believe that I'd still be alive and moving when the sun rose.

I pulled out the water bottle, my hand moving so slowly it made me impatient. I took a mouthful of water and held it. Its coolness soothed my raw mouth and tongue, but I didn't swallow.

It helped me to get started walking through the shadowy night.

8
Moon Visions

I WALKED INTO THE EYE OF THE MOON. AT TIMES IT almost blinded me, though it was reddish and only partly there. Still, it gave me light to find my way. The night was wonderfully cool. My skin was chilly, and I was glad of it. After the searing I'd had for days, it would take a long time for cold to bother me.

I came to the end of the tabletop mesa. It slanted away southeast, following the course of all the ranges in this part of the country. I could have stayed on its top and gone almost the way I wanted to, but it was so uneven and cut with gullies that I decided to go down. It was just as easy, and I could keep the moon at the same angle to my course, as long as it was still in the east.

I found a track down the steep side of the mountain, though it was really more illusion than anything else. In the moonlight it was shadowed, which made it seem deep and safe, and I set off along it with a confidence that something inside me knew was false. Another part of me didn't care, though. That was the part that had been listening, feeling the air and sensing the wind.

Was that what Nachito had meant? I seemed to feel every stir of life among the rocks. Pocket gophers, lizards, scorpions, packrats, all were going about their business for the night, and something inside me knew all about them. I could sense something huge and menacing, just over the horizon. I understood that it was the world I'd known all my days, felt through the perceptions of other kinds of life. It was an eery feeling, as if there were two of me.

The moon tugged me onward. I set my gaze on it, though I knew very well that was a foolish thing to do. I felt someone near me. The moon's face blurred, and Dad was looking at me.

"Good boy, Burr!" he said. "I knew you had it in you. Keep at it, if you die trying!" Then he was gone. I found myself standing on the little path with my eyes full of tears.

I blinked very hard. The glare of the moon had dazzled me, and I couldn't see ahead. I didn't dare move forward until I had my night-vision back, for the trail I was following was too sketchy to chance going it blind. I stood still, letting the chilly breeze bring the high, clean scents of the mountains to my nose. I wondered, for one instant, how it would smell to a cougar.

As I stood, eyes closed, that strange sense returned to me. I could feel small creatures scurrying about on the mountainside and among the rocks. A screech overhead told me some airborne predator was at work. An owl? There were trees enough on some of the ridges I'd seen from the top of the mesa to support owls, maybe. A muffled rattle in the pebbles of the path a bit ahead told me a snake was moving on its way.

I opened my eyes. I could see again, and this time I kept my gaze on the path, knowing the moon's position from the shadows of rocks.

It was a long way down. Twice I almost took a header straight down, as bits of the loose rubble gave way beneath my feet. No matter that it was cold, I was sweating by the time I came to a long, flat stretch, almost like a porch laid along the side of the mesa. There were trees, piñons and juniper I thought from the smell, tucked in at its edge against the cliff. I knew I'd never find a better place to rest. My legs were shaking with fatigue, and the rest of me wasn't much better.

The night was never still. Anybody who thought of this as deserted country, looking at it on a map, just hadn't been here at night. It was alive with creatures. I leaned against the rough bark of a scrubby juniper and listened. Even wild things were company, when you were alone.

I rubbed my eyes. My fingers were gritty and made them sting. It seemed strange that I hadn't spoken to anybody, any human being, since that last farewell to Dad. And Dad had been dead then. I wondered if that counted. I shook my head. My wits were getting fuzzy.

I struggled to my feet after a while and decided I'd better move while I could. I had no idea of how far I'd come or how far I still had to go. But I knew I'd better keep moving. To stay still for too long was to die. I knew that without any doubt.

"I'm no Apache!" I protested aloud. All the small sounds hushed at once.

I sighed and took up my long trek again. This time my eyes kept turning toward the moon so persistently that I gave up trying to keep them from it. My feet were feeling their way along, but my mind floated above . . . far above. I was filled with reddish moonlight, though the moon was now overhead and didn't stare into my eyes.

Something hauled me to a stop, one foot still

raised to step. My head was spinning, and I was shaking again. All over, this time. I took out my bottle of water for a sip, and my hand froze where it was.

The cougar was standing on the pathway, facing me. The track was so uneven, up and down, that I was a bit lower than he was, though he was farther on. Looking up, I could see the big cat against the moon. It was outlined in a nimbus of cold fire, and from the dark face glowed two eyes like coals.

I waited to become terrified. I should have. But instead there came a sense of companionship. Not the chummy kind, far from it. Instead, an appraising sort of feeling that grew stronger as the cat looked me over. Then it raised its head and squalled.

I don't know how long I stood there in the path. The cougar went away, and I didn't move. When I really came to, the moon was past being overhead. Its light shone directly onto the path now, and I could see, just where the cat had stood, a gaping gully, cut sharply at an angle across the track. If I had walked on blindly, I'd have gone right into it.

The moonlight was bright, and I knelt to look for any trace of the big cat. There wasn't a pawprint to be seen. There was no wild smell on the night air. Had it been real, that panther? Or had my own mind warned me? Was I hallucinating then? Or now?

I stared down into those black depths, pitched a pebble into the darkness. After a long time a tiny clatter came back to my ears. It was real.

This was three times. First I'd seen the print of that big paw in the sand of the streambed. I'd heard the cries and seen the tawny shape for an instant after I'd reached the top of the chimney. Now this.

Something came to me. Charlie had longed for a strong sign for his own medicine journey. A totem of great power. What could be stronger than a cougar? Was this my totemic beast?

"You're getting lightheaded," I told myself. "It's safer not to keep going, if you're going to get all nutty."

I stopped where I was and propped myself against a boulder. Cold as I soon was, I slept until daylight woke me.

9
"Keep Going, Burr!"

THE DRIED FRUIT WAS ALL GONE. THE WATER BOTTLE had only a small slosh left in it. My head felt swollen, light and dry; and my feet were so badly cut and bruised that I just put them out of my mind. I couldn't do a thing for them, and they had to keep going, no matter what. Only the tops of my tennies remained, tied about my ankles to do what they could to keep my insteps from being cooked by the sun. I'd looked back once, and there had been blood where I stepped. I didn't look back anymore.

More than once I had come to and found myself lying full-length on the ground. Sometimes it was in the shadow of a boulder. Sometimes it was out in the full blaze of the sun. I must be blacking out, but I didn't know what to do about that, either.

At the moment I felt pretty clearheaded. I was on the top of another mesa, looking down into a long valley. There was foliage down there at its bottom. I hadn't seen that much green for a long time. Maybe water . . . ?

I almost started scrambling down the slope toward a ledge that looked to be a possible path. Then I stopped. That wasn't the way. The breeze whispered its disapproval. Charlie wouldn't do it that way. Dad wouldn't. Nachito most certainly wouldn't. You didn't dive head first down a mountain to get water.

"Control!" I croaked to myself. "Only way . . . control. One step at a time."

That seemed terribly funny, though sensible, and I smiled. My face almost cracked off when my mouth moved. I looked along the flattish place where I stood. Up ahead was a crack. Maybe an animal trail, going down to water in the valley below.

If there was water.

I limped on, picking my way carefully, and found a notch where a dizzy trail looped off down the side of the mesa. Nachito stood there, nodding in his judicious way.

"Yes. That is the way. Only white men go running off after matters they do not understand. The Apache go step by step, seeing everything, learning all. There is no room here for an accident or a mistake. You are making a good Apache, Burr. If you keep at it for a couple of lifetimes, you may become one of the People."

It didn't seem a bit strange that the old Indian was there. I nodded as I passed the spot where he had stood, but he was gone. I fitted my feet cautiously into the narrow slot of the path and didn't look down. I'd learned about that early in this game. Instead, I kept my gaze fixed on the meandering path, searching out any place where the edge was weathering away enough to send me down with a crumble of rock.

There was a rattling buzz somewhere in the hot brightness. This time it didn't congeal my insides. The snake belonged here, I didn't.

"Just passing through," I said. My voice sounded slurred, even to me. "No problem. Keep your scales on." I didn't pick up my pace, just kept going easily. The rattle died away. No sting of fangs in my calf. I'd made it past still another hurdle. Somehow I'd come to a kind of understanding with the snakes. Or I was getting lucky, at this late date.

Halfway down I had to stop and burrow under a scrubby bush for some rest. My muscles had turned to water. My knees were wavering under me like reeds in a high wind. And my head—even the handkerchief hat wasn't doing much good.

I sprawled on my face in the hot grit. Every spot on my back where the sun struck through the skimpy leaves burned separately. I'd never thought of the sun as my worst enemy, but it was. Worse than any rattler. Worse by far than the cougar.

I found myself wondering where the beast might be, right now. Lying up, cool and comfortable in his lair, I supposed.

I lay there for a long time, letting my body go limp, though my legs kept jerking from time to time. Every time I almost fell asleep, I'd fall through space and end up with a bump that woke me again. My mind kept running at top speed all the time, too. Asleep or awake or halfway between, nightmares kept acting themselves out behind my eyes.

I fell down the chimney, head first, and smashed against the rubble at its bottom. The first snake didn't relax and go away, but bit me and left me rolling in dying agony on the stony slope. The plane crash killed me, along with Dad.

Dad . . .

"Get up, Burr! Keep going! This isn't getting you anywhere. So you're tired? I'm *dead*, for cat's sake, and I'm still in here pitching! Come on, haul yourself up and get this show on the road!"

"I can't be an Apache, Dad." I rolled onto my hands and knees, then rose painfully to my feet. "I can use some things they did, but I'm not one. Does that make a difference?"

"They were tough, smart, efficient. They lived where few others could have. But we can be just as tough and smart, Burr. We don't often have to; but when it's necessary, we can do it. Now shag it!"

And he was gone. But I was on my feet. The sun was down a bit behind the distant top of the mesa. The wind was coming up the slope from the valley. It seemed a fraction cooler than it had.

After a dreamlike time I found myself at the foot of the steep. I didn't remember anything along the way. I must've done the last miles on automatic pilot. That was scary.

The valley was narrow. I staggered across sun-killed grass toward a line of gray-green cottonwoods. There had to be a creek there! There just had to be!

The wide, flat streambed was bone dry.

10
Thinking It Out

I DROPPED ONTO MY KNEES AND SCRABBLED FRANTI-cally with both hands, skinning my knuckles on stones, tearing my fingernails. The ground wasn't even damp, no matter how I dug. It had been a long time since the last rain.

I went back onto my heels. At least I was in the shade, and coolness had crept into the bowl between the mountains as the sun went down.

I searched among the round pebbles in the creek bottom until I found one twice the size of a Life Saver, then scrubbed off the grit onto my T-shirt. It was so ragged and dirty Mom wouldn't have used it for cleaning rags. When I put the stone into my mouth, a bit of saliva began collecting around it, as the glands went to work. It was like Nachito had said . . . it helped, but not much.

I looked up the shaded curve where the creek should have been running. There was no hint that any dampness was left anywhere. The plants that had grown along the stream were dried to straw.

I could waste precious time searching for water, but I had a gut feeling that I wouldn't find any. And I surely didn't have the energy to waste. Besides, I still had a swallow or two in the bottle.

I shook the container without opening it. For the last day or two I'd managed to carry a mouthful for a long time before swallowing any of it. Now I had control of things when it came to quenching my thirst. As for hunger . . . the thought of food made me faintly nauseated. Except for the weakness in my legs, the swimming sensation in my head, that no longer bothered me at all.

I crouched there sucking the pebble, my mind busy. It was going to be tight. I still hadn't a clue as to where I might be. I knew I was well east of my original location, but as I didn't know precisely where that was, it didn't help much. And what with blackouts and walking on auto-pilot, I might have wandered all over the map.

Yet I still had some strength. A little energy, if I was careful. In this situation Nachito would probably stroll on home and go dancing tonight. I wasn't that lucky. The strenuous training the old Apache had had was lacking, despite my time with Charlie.

I creaked to my feet and looked up the slope waiting on the other side of the valley. An easy one, this time. It slanted gradually up toward a cap of boulders that glowed red in the sunset. If I could make it up there, I'd spend the night in that clump of rock. I should be able to see quite a distance. Maybe there would be the light of a ranch, or at least a house. Maybe I would see a road or a cow, or something.

I felt something staring at my back. Turning slowly, I stared behind. A cougar stood there, watching me with interest from the cottonwoods. It was smaller than the first, I thought. More gray than tantawny. I stared back at it.

I wasn't afraid. Not at all. I'd had to worry about too many kinds of death to feel anything about this. I didn't move. It was as if my real self was floating several feet above where my body was standing. I was watching what happened, seeing the boy and the cat staring at each other in the twilight. My mind was mildly curious, nothing more.

The animal gave a low rumble. It wasn't threatening . . . curious, too, maybe. I saw it turn in its tracks and stalk away among the cottonwoods. Only then did I crank up enough breath to utter a long, "Whooosh!"

I went up the rise in record time, my adrenals finally coming to attention. At the boulders, I sang out to them, "Impulse power all the way!"

The tumble of huge stones was warm from the sun, as I dropped to the ground and leaned against one. That was good. It was now getting very cold again. It seemed as if I were either getting roasted or frozen, no happy medium.

When I had my breath back, I looked around, then climbed onto the tallest spur of rock to look better. There wasn't a light to be seen, except for a glare against the sky that had to come from a town. A reddish light, it shone against some high cirrus clouds. Over there, then, was the way to go. I drew a long mark in the dust, with an arrowhead pointing in the right direction.

Lying with my feet close to that mark, I knew I should be sleeping, but I was thinking again. That cougar . . . it had to be a different one. Not the same I'd seen so far to the west.

"No single beast is the sign," came Nachito's voice in the light breeze. "When you have need, the animal appears. That is your proof; all that anyone should need. He is your guide and your protector. He will kill you, in his single animal shape, if that is how it turns out. But if you pay heed to the things he tells you, shows you, warns you about, then you can survive."

Those words came straight out of my memory. Nachito had spoken them to Charlie, there in his little house with me, all ears, sitting beside the table with the family.

I wondered sleepily what Nachito would name me after my Medicine Walk. When I got home. If I got home. Surely a cougar should put some zip into my name.

I yawned, almost swallowed the pebble, and spat it into my hand. I put it away carefully for future use. My mouth felt like an old boot that had been left outside for years until it cracked into dusty strips, but the pebble had helped some. I wouldn't risk swallowing it; it might not do my insides any harm, but I wanted it for tomorrow. It was just the right size and shape.

I leaned against the warm rock, curled my feet, now feeling half frozen, under myself. Suddenly I was asleep.

11
Feelings Don't
Amount to Much

THE NEXT MORNING WAS A BLUR. I FOUND A PIÑON and chewed on needles for my breakfast. I took a tiny sip of water. I shook myself vigorously, trying to make my body feel as if it were alive. Then I dared to look into the bottle to see how much water was left. There might be half a teacup in it.

I stared down at the arrow I'd drawn the night before. It pointed off into what seemed empty country . . . but I had seen those lights. There had to be something there, beyond the heights and valleys. I checked the angle of the sun, looked around for something tall enough to give me a reference point. I knew I'd have to pick up new ones as I moved down into lower country, but I picked a point that would give me something to keep my bearings by for a while at least.

Only then did I take a cautious mouthful from the bottle and settle it comfortably around my tongue. Once I began walking again, the liquid warmed rapidly in my mouth. I moved slowly, looking back at those boulders often, making certain I was headed right. My feet weren't altogether sure on the rough terrain, and my head was feeling light again.

The land slanted, but the downward slope was less abrupt than some I'd traveled. That helped a little, for a while. By noon I was down in another canyon, threading my way among fallen boulders. A long angle of scree seemed to promise a way out, further along in the direction I wanted to go.

I tried to sort things out as I walked. Was it four days or five? I seemed to have been climbing and walking and trying for years. I counted backward. I could remember four . . . no, five . . . nights spent curled against rocks or in hollows or in a tree. For the past day and a half there'd been nothing to eat. I didn't trust my memory about edible insects, and the plants in this area were different from those at home. To get sick now was to die, and I knew it.

As the sun roasted me, drying my flesh onto my bones, I found myself wanting to give up. The water had been swallowed for a long time. I hurt in everything I owned. It would be so nice to say, "I can't do any more. I've given it my best shot, but this is as far as I can go." Then I'd lie down in some shady spot and wait for things to end.

The tiny slosh left in the bottle wouldn't even make a mouthful to travel on. I was done. Every bone I had screamed for me to stop, to give up, to accept whatever might come.

I thought about doing just that as I crawled and slid and scrambled up the loose scree, stones sliding down behind me to the canyon's floor. But I was like a steak on Dad's outdoor grill. This wasn't a good place to die, out here in the sun with nothing but shattered rocks all around. I'd get to the top. Then I'd quit.

Once there I uncapped the bottle and drank the rest of the water. Might as well die with a wet throat. Then I looked around.

I was on a high roll of land that ridged off into a maze of other ridges and canyons. There were trees near by. Real trees. Water?

I couldn't find a drop. But at least there was shade. Shade to die in. I found a likely spot and lay full-length beneath the shelter of dusty green branches. I closed my eyes. All I had to do was wait. Dad would come for me, after a while. Maybe Mom would come, too.

"So you feel tired and hot and thirsty and hungry?" That was Nachito's sharp old voice in my ear. "That is really *tough*! How do you think those Apache felt when Geronimo took them from the government camp and ran them across the desert? Over fifty miles, it was! Mostly women and children, too, and old people. They were gone before the cavalry knew anything was up."

"But they were Apache!" I protested, opening my eyes. I didn't see Nachito, but the waspish voice didn't stop talking.

"They were human. They weren't up against a life or death situation. They could have stayed where they were, starving and sick, begging for scraps of rotten meat from the white men. But they saw a vision of freedom, and they went after it. Just freedom, White-Eye. Not survival. They gambled everything they had. Some of them won."

I rolled over onto my stomach and covered my ears with my hands. That didn't help a bit.

"So your feelings are all shot, are they? The People know how to turn off their feelings. That was why the whites thought us so cruel. We didn't let ourselves feel anything except the one thing toward which we aimed. Feelings don't amount to much, Burr Henderson. They're a luxury for people who don't have to scrounge and strain and dig to survive.

If you're going to let something silly like feelings make you lie down and die, then I'm through with you. Charlie knows better. I thought you'd been around him and me enough to learn that."

I sighed and sat up. My head was clearer than it had been for a long time.

"I guess I must have been around Charlie and his grandfather long enough to pick up *something*," I said aloud. A startled lizard took flight. "They won't let me give up and die."

I groaned and stood. The bottle weighed more than it had when it was full. I almost threw it away, but I tucked it into the pouch with the flash and bandages. I might need it later. I might find water. I knew I wouldn't stop again. Nachito wouldn't let me.

I looked back across the canyon I'd come through. In the distance I could see that distinctive pile of rocks. I looked in the direction I was going. Off there was a town. I found an irregular peak I thought might stay in sight for a while and started off again.

My feet were terrible. My head throbbed with heat and dizziness. I felt as if I might stumble and fall and be totally unable to move, no matter how Nachito scolded.

Just feelings. What if I were carrying a couple of babies? Running for all I was worth to get away from the conditions Nachito had told me about in the government camps for Apache? Soldiers pursuing . . . and they wouldn't mind killing me, no matter if I were a woman or child, man or baby, old or young.

As I went, I turned off feelings, one set at a time. Feet? Scratch feet. My mind blanked out that set of pains. Legs? Ditto.

Up my body I went, erasing any signals my nerves were sending to my brain. When I finished, I felt like a robot, stalking along on metal pads. I didn't need anything but an occasional grease job and maybe a jolt of electricity every thousand miles. The idea struck me as very funny, and I laughed as I walked, my throat cracking.

"I'm a Burr-bot!" I shouted. My face cracked, too. "I'll make it now!"

12
The Trek of
the Burr-Bot

IT WAS A STRANGE WAY TO TRAVEL—OR TO EXIST, FOR that matter. I felt as if I might be, once more, several feet above myself, looking down on the dusty boy with stumbling feet and pounding head. Once I had cut myself away from the things my physical body was trying to tell me, my mind was cool and clear.

Once I'd had one of those radio-controlled little planes. This was a lot like that: I'd send the signal down, when I noticed an obstacle up ahead. "Body, bear right at the big rock!" Or, "There's a rattler to your right, behind the melon-sized stone. Keep left!" The body down there would obey, and I didn't have to live inside the thing.

But I knew it couldn't last forever. Even Nachito couldn't run things from up above for very long at a time. With one fringe of my mind I knew that that body down there was losing fluid at an alarming rate. By the time this day was over, I'd be a dried-out husk, lost in the rubble of some canyon, or lying on some mesa for the vultures to quarrel over. But I'd have died trying. There was a lot of satisfaction in that.

Dad would be proud, when he came to meet me. Mom would quirk her mouth in that crooked smile of hers and tousle my hair and say, "Good show, Robert Burr Henderson!" It would be fine. I only had to keep myself going to that point.

I kept losing my reference points. Going up and down and around kept getting me behind high places, where I lost them. I'd come out of a canyon and look around, and the sun would be in the wrong quarter of the sky. If I didn't keep my wits about me, I was going to get turned around and miss my goal entirely.

It was late in the day. I hadn't dropped yet. I was still trudging along when I realized that I wasn't stumbling and scrambling. I was on the side of a mountain. To my left was a sheer drop. To the right was a weather-gnawed cliff. And beneath my feet—I stopped and stared hard—was a road. Well-defined. Not paved, of course, that would have been ridiculous, but there were double wheel tracks. At some time a grader had come along and cut a flat shelf into the slope.

The sun was down and had been for some time.

There was still light lying in streaks across the valley; the shapes of peaks to west were outlined in shadow on the lower ground and on the ridges rising beyond. It would be dark soon, but now I had something to follow. Roads went someplace, that was their only reason for existing.

My legs buckled under me, dumping me down into the dust of the road. I came to myself with a thump. All my aches and pains came back at once. There wasn't an inch of me that didn't hurt, inside or out. My heart was thudding fit to burst my chest open. Everything turned dark behind my eyes.

Was this it, after I'd worked so hard and almost made it?

"NO!" I shouted. My voice wasn't even a good croak. Hardly more than a whisper. But I passed out anyway.

It was pitch dark when I came to. I checked to make sure I still hurt—that meant I wasn't dead—and struggled up to a sitting position. There were stars up there. The moon, rising later every night, wasn't yet up. But I could see a bit. I tried to stand and couldn't. I hadn't been any weaker after I'd had pneumonia and been in bed for weeks. My head was spinning, and I sat still to let it stop.

While I sat there in the darkness, the cougar's tawny face rose up into my mind. It seemed to be smiling a smug cat smile, the whiskers twitching a bit, the forehead wrinkled. Then, with a purring growl, it winked out. I heaved myself to my feet.

I knew which way to go, for once. Downhill on that road! It had to lead into the valley I'd seen earlier. I had to stay on the road . . . or fall off the edge. There was no alternative.

I lifted one heavy, cooked-hamburger foot and set it it in the track. I lifted the other and pushed it ahead of the first. Another step. Another. Step after step I shoved myself along the road, toward whatever waited at its end.

13
The Apache

I ALMOST WALKED STRAIGHT INTO THE HOUSE. THE
road had gotten wider as it went, until it shelved out
and became part of the valley's floor. Once that happened it wasn't easy to keep right in the track. I'd
been bumbling around when I walked full-tilt into a
cottonwood tree. The familiar dusty scent told me
what it was, and another whiff assured me that I must
be near water. Then I could see the side of a small
house, shining dimly in the starlight. I thought it
might be adobe, from the look of it.

I sagged against the tree. "Hello?" I yelled. It
didn't carry two feet.

I tried to clear my throat, to bring my croak's
volume up some. "Hey there! Is anybody home?"
This time some sound came out.

It was answered by another inside the hut. Someone fumbled around. There was the scritch of a match. A reddish light made a square puddle on the ground in front of the low doorway.

"Who is there?" The words were accompanied by the sound of the safety catch being clicked off on a rifle.

"Jus' me. Burr . . . Hen . . . der . . . son . . ." And everything went really black for a long time.

I woke lying on a pile of blankets. They smelled as if they'd been packed away for a long time. It wasn't really light in the room, but I could see enough to know that daylight had come, outside. And that I was in a cramped space with adobe walls. Sitting cross-legged, facing me, was an Indian. He was watching me closely, his dark, narrow face as expressionless as Nachito's. I hadn't the faintest doubt in the world that he was Apache.

He didn't say anything when he saw me watching him. He bent and took up a cup of water that had been sitting on a stool beside him. He held it out and tilted it so I could get my mouth on its rim—that's how small the room was. There wasn't much water in the cup, and I understood why.

I licked my cracked lips. That doesn't begin to describe them. Burned, split, raw, bleeding: those words don't even start on how they felt. But I made them shape words.

"Don't worry. I won't drink much. I know all

about drinking too much after going without water for a long time. Nachito taught me." I found with some surprise that I now had a voice. The Apache must have dribbled water into me while I slept. My tongue wasn't nearly as stiff as it had been.

"Nachito?" His voice was deep, quiet, very educated. "My father knew such a one, when he was a boy. Nachito went out to work on the ranches."

I stared at him. "Could be the same one. He works . . . worked . . . for my dad as foreman of our little spread down to the southwest." Suddenly I felt tears coming into my eyes, no matter how I struggled to stop them. Now I knew, all the way down, that Dad was dead. There was no deadly battle of survival to hold the knowledge away any longer.

"Dad died, you know. Had a heart attack, I think, and put our plane down before he . . . went. He's back there, somewhere, still in the plane." Something got in the way of my voice, and I had to gulp. But somehow I didn't feel ashamed of it.

The man rose effortlessly on short, strong legs. "You might like something to eat. Once I saw you, I knew you couldn't handle anything solid, so I boiled up some broth. It's lucky I killed a jackrabbit yesterday—they're tough, but they make good soup." He went into the darkness at the back of the hut, and I could hear him moving around.

By the time he came back with a bowl and spoon, I had the tears dried and my voice in working order again. I wanted to talk to this man, tell him all about the strange things that had happened to me on that long walk through the mountains and across the rough country. Even with my mouth full, I kept babbling on, pouring it all out. At the end I said, surprised, "And I think it was the People who kept me going. The People and the cougar. Between them, they kept pushing, wouldn't let me quit. Nachito stood there and blessed me out, when he needed to."

The seamed face cracked into a smile. He stretched out his hand to me. "I am Miguel," he said. "I, too, am of the People. Or perhaps I should say that I am a descendant of them. We have lost much of what we were and what we knew. Few of the young people in my own family could have made the walk that you have made, accomplished the things you have accomplished. The few who have made their own Medicine Walks will honor you, when I tell them of this. There are few who will push themselves, endure the pain of acquiring the old strengths.

"You found, it may be, some trace of the truly Old Ones, up there in the high places where they loved to live. There was enough of the teaching in you for you to respond to them, perhaps. I wonder how many Apache, nowadays, would do as well . . ."

He put away the empty bowl, wiped the spoon on a cloth and set it on a shelf.

"I come here sometimes, when I want to get away from the town, the quarreling of people who know better, the stinks of cars and asphalt. If you had come this morning, I would have been gone; I intended to start out at daylight. It's a good thing you came when you did; it is fifteen miles to the next inhabited place."

I rolled off the pile of blankets and pushed myself upright with my hands. "Ooooof! Everything I own hurts!" I groaned. Then what the man had said penetrated.

"I passed out, up there someplace. Didn't come to until after dark. The cougar came . . . not really. In my mind. If he hadn't, I might have stayed there until morning. He made me come down. Do you think . . . ?"

Miguel shrugged. "Who knows, with the Old Ones? Your people would say that you hallucinated. Mine would say that your guiding spirit moved your feet and supported your will. Who is to say which is right? Or that both are not the same thing, put into different terms?"

14

Grampa

IT WASN'T LONG BEFORE MIGUEL DECIDED I WAS FIT
to travel and loaded me into his antique pickup, along
with his camping gear and lots of books. He stopped
at the first tiny settlement, which wasn't much more
than a combination gas station and grocery store.

"I'll call from here," he said. "No use letting
your grandfather suffer longer than necessary. Then
I'll take you on into town. It will take us so long to
nurse Bertha here along these roads that he'll probably be waiting for us . . . if he can get a charter
promptly. Small planes aren't always easy to come by
on short notice."

I didn't get out of the pickup. I was so tired that
it seemed as if my bones had melted. Nothing could
excite me much. I nodded and tucked my feet up on

the ragged seat of the pickup. My knee hit something hard, and I ran my hand under the red blanket covering it. It was another book.

The title jumped out at me. *The Totemic Beast: Rites of Adolescence* was printed in gold above the name of the author. Miguel Corona Sanches.

I could hardly wait until he came out of the store and cranked up Bertha. "Did you write this?" I asked, holding out the book.

He grinned, his cheeks creasing into long lines. "Yes. That is one of mine."

"But you're Apache. Why the Spanish name?"

"My family chose it when the whites demanded family names of us. Most Apache spoke Spanish before learning English, away back. It was easiest. Our real names . . . the Apache ones . . . we keep to ourselves." He steered around a boulder that had tumbled from the cliff onto the roadway. "I teach in a university. I'm on sabbatical leave right now. For a year. It would have been years, maybe, before I came back to camp in my old hut. My leave is up this weekend. Makes you think, doesn't it?"

It did. But something had me thinking hard. "Was this my rite of adolescence?" I asked him. "Some Indian tribes sent their boys out to fast and pray and wait for a sign that would give them a name for their adult lives. Was that what I did? I had no idea of doing that when I started. I didn't want to. But was that what really happened?"

Miguel shrugged. The old pickup rocked from side to side along the rutted track. "*Quien sabe?* Nobody nowadays takes such things seriously. But it worked, whatever it was. You have your name. You are now a man, no matter that you were a boy just a few days ago. You have earned a name, by all my people's rules."

"What is it?" I asked him. Something terrifically excited was fluttering in my stomach. "Tell me, please!"

He looked over at me, his brows raised. "I can't do that. Only the one who lived it all, saw the visions, felt the sun, dreamed the dreams, can do that. *You* tell *me!*"

I swallowed hard. Then I thought for a long time, as the truck jounced along. There were so many things to think about. I'd learned from people like Dad and Nachito and Charlie. I'd learned from that first snake, from the wind and the rock and the few plants. But most of all I'd learned from the cougar. It had prodded me at all the right times. It would take a while to figure out what my name might be, but I knew without a doubt what my totem was.

We pulled into a small, dusty town about noon, and Miguel stopped at a Dairy Queen. He brought back two huge chocolate milkshakes. I hadn't thought I was hungry until the first cold, thick, chocolatey glob slid down my throat. I'd never tasted anything so good in all my life.

We drove on toward the airport, where a limp wind sock hung from a mast on the single hangar. We parked in the shade of the Quonset-type terminal and asked at the desk inside if Grampa had arrived yet.

Before the girl could answer, there came a hail from the back of the building, and Grampa limped forward from the worn couch where he'd been sitting with his head below the level of the front counter.

"Burr! My boy, come here. Let me make sure I'm not fooling myself again!" He held out his arms, and I dived into them. For the first time in almost a week I was where I belonged, with my own family. I felt his heart thumping beneath his cotton shirt, and I knew my own was keeping time with his. When he let me go, finally, I stepped back and looked up into his face. His white moustache was bristling the way it does when he doesn't want to show his feelings. He was looking over my head toward Miguel.

"Dwight?" he asked in a small, quiet voice. "You didn't mention him when you called . . ." Miguel shook his head, his face sad.

Grampa straightened his back. His eyes shone bright with tears for a second, then they were dry again. I could use that trick. My own face was wet.

When Grampa reached out to me again, I let it go. I really cried, as I'd needed to do for so long. When I was done, I wiped off the wet on Grampa's shirt before coming up for air. I felt a lot better, though I knew that cold lump would be inside me for a long, long time.

I finally remembered my manners and said, "Grampa, this is Miguel Sanches. He teaches in a university and writes books. And rescues me."

Grampa reached out his hand and took Miguel's. Neither of them spoke for a moment.

Then Miguel smiled. "You are together, now. With family, which is a good feeling, as I know too well. My address is in this book . . ." He held out *Rites of Adolescence*. ". . . which I think you have earned. Write to me. Tell me anything you remember, as time goes along. I will be more than interested. But now I must go. I have to be back at work on Monday."

I looked at Grampa, who fumbled in his wallet and took out one of his cards. "You can reach us here, any time. The boy may want to live with us, or he may want to go back to the ranch. That'll be up to him. He's always been pretty levelheaded. I can see that he's grown up since I saw him last, too. But you can reach him through me. Thank you, sir.

You little know what comfort you have brought to an old man and his wife."

Miguel shook hands again, turned and went to Bertha. The pickup started in a cloud of smoke and left in a storm of fumes mingled with dust. I stared after him, feeling somehow lost.

Beyond the road the mountains loomed, distant and dim. Up there I'd left the Burr Henderson I had been all my life. He hadn't been a bad fellow. I'd liked him pretty well, all things considered. I felt a tug inside me. I could see a deep canyon, a tawny flicker of motion. I shook myself.

"I've got to write him soon. I know my name. It has to be Learned from the Cougar," I said to Grampa, who looked puzzled.

"What's that all about?" he asked me.

Suddenly I was ravenously hungry. "Does this dump have a lunch counter?" I asked. He nodded, and I tugged him toward it.

"I'll tell you all about it, Grampa, while we eat. Right now it's just struck me that I'm starving. Do you mind if I talk with my mouth full?"

Mom would have killed me, but I talked around and through the hamburger and fries, all the time we ate. Grampa was astonished, shocked, concerned . . . all the right responses. But I found myself not quite satisfied. Miguel had understood everything, down to his toenails. Nachito and Charlie would, too, when I had a chance to talk to them.

I knew, with a kind of sadness, that only another one of the People would really comprehend what it was I was saying.

But I smiled at Grampa and kept on talking.

Postscript

IF ANYBODY WONDERS, I WENT BACK TO THE RANCH to live, with Nachito and Charlie right at hand. Mom's cousin, Sidney Farrell, had just been laid off his job in Detroit—he's an automotive engineer—and was looking for something to do. Grampa fixed it up for him to bring his family out and live with me and look after things until the will gets settled and things sort of simmer down.

I like Sidney, and even his daughters are not too bad, as little kids go. I can see that they're young enough to teach, if I get started right with them. His wife doesn't much like living in the West, but she's all right and will adjust, I think.

Dad left trusts set up, with guardians and that sort of thing. I'll probably end up living with Nachito and his son and family. That's what I'd like. Sidney and his bunch can have the big house for as long as they like.

Charlie and I are being taught together, now. Nachito admits that I may not have to live more than a century to make one of the People. I'm gaining on it!